Sep[...]
To Room 4AM

From

Alexandra Framer

I Went to the Zoo

by RITA GOLDEN GELMAN
illustrated by MARYANN KOVALSKI

SCHOLASTIC HARDCOVER

SCHOLASTIC INC.
New York

Library of Congress Cataloging-in-Publication Data
Gelman, Rita Golden.
I went to the zoo / written by Rita Golden Gelman;
illustrated by Maryann Kovalski.
p.   cm.
Summary: Thinking that the zoo animals look "as bored
as bored could be," a boy takes them all home with him.
ISBN 0-590-45882-5
[1. Zoos — Fiction. 2. Stories in rhyme.]
I. Kovalski, Maryann, ill. II. Title.
PZ8.3.G28Iam   1993
[E] — dc20   92-27671   CIP
AC

12 11 10 9 8 7 6 5 4 3 2 1   3 4 5 6 7 8/9

Printed in the U.S.A.   36

First Scholastic printing, September 1993

Book design by Kristina Iulo

For the paintings in this book,
the illustrator used gouache
and colored pencil.

For Carolina, Francisco,
Carlos, and Isabel Restrepo,
Juan and Carolina Blanco Restrepo,
and their wonderful *abuela,*
Amparo Jaramillo.

R.G.G.

To Jenny, Joanna, and Gregory.

M.K.

The other day I went to the zoo.

I don't know why I went to the zoo.
It was a silly thing to do.
 The pandas were sitting.
 The camels were spitting.
They were as bored as bored could be.
"Come home," I said. "Come home
with me."

PLEASE
DON'T

The other day I went to the zoo.
I don't know why I went to the zoo.
It was a silly thing to do.
  The monkeys were swinging.
  Koalas were clinging.
  The pandas were sitting.
  The camels were spitting.
They were as bored as bored could be.
"Come home," I said. "Come home
with me."

PLEASE
DON'T FEED

The other day I went to the zoo.
I don't know why I went to the zoo.
It was a silly thing to do.
   The rabbits were hopping.
   The pigs were slopping.
   The monkeys were swinging.
   Koalas were clinging.
   The pandas were sitting.
   The camels were spitting.
They were as bored as bored could be.
"Come home," I said. "Come home
with me."

PLEASE
DON'T FEED

The other day I went to the zoo.
I don't know why I went to the zoo.
It was a silly thing to do.
 The penguins were sliding,
 The ostriches hiding.
 The rabbits were hopping.
 The pigs were slopping.
 The monkeys were swinging.
 Koalas were clinging.
 The pandas were sitting.
 The camels were spitting.
They were as bored as bored could be.
"Come home," I said. "Come home
with me."

PLEASE
DON'T FEED

The other day I went to the zoo.
I don't know why I went to the zoo.
It was a silly thing to do.
　　The horses were neighing,
　　The mantises praying.
　　The penguins were sliding,
　　The ostriches hiding.
　　The rabbits were hopping.
　　The pigs were slopping.
　　The monkeys were swinging.
　　Koalas were clinging.
　　The pandas were sitting.
　　The camels were spitting.
They were as bored as bored could be.
"Come home," I said. "Come home
with me."

PLEASE
DON'T FEED

The other day I went to the zoo.
I don't know why I went to the zoo.
It was a silly thing to do.
    The hippos were soaking.
    The bullfrogs were croaking.
    The horses were neighing,
    The mantises praying.
    The penguins were sliding,
    The ostriches hiding.
    The rabbits were hopping.
    The pigs were slopping.
    The monkeys were swinging.
    Koalas were clinging.
    The pandas were sitting.
    The camels were spitting.
They were as bored as bored could be.
"Come home," I said. "Come home
with me."

PRAYING
MANTIS
(LOOK CLOSE)

The other day I went to the zoo.
I don't know why I went to the zoo.
It was a silly thing to do.
  The beavers were slapping.
  The seals were clapping.
  The hippos were soaking.
  The bullfrogs were croaking.
  The horses were neighing,
  The mantises praying.
  The penguins were sliding,
  The ostriches hiding.
  The rabbits were hopping.
  The pigs were slopping.
  The monkeys were swinging.
  Koalas were clinging.
  The pandas were sitting.
  The camels were spitting.
They were as bored as bored could be.
"Come home," I said. "Come home
with me."

The other day I went to the zoo.
I don't know why I went to the zoo.
It was a silly thing to do.

 The tigers were crouching,
 The kangaroos pouching.
 The beavers were slapping.
 The seals were clapping.
 The hippos were soaking.
 The bullfrogs were croaking.
 The horses were neighing,
 The mantises praying.
 The penguins were sliding,
 The ostriches hiding.
 The rabbits were hopping.
 The pigs were slopping.
 The monkeys were swinging.
 Koalas were clinging.
 The pandas were sitting.
 The camels were spitting.
They were as bored as bored could be.
"Come home," I said. "Come home
with me."

The other day I went to the zoo.
I don't know why I went to the zoo.
It was a silly thing to do.
   The peacocks were posing,
   The elephants hosing.
   The tigers were crouching,
   The kangaroos pouching.
   The beavers were slapping.
   The seals were clapping.
   The hippos were soaking.
   The bullfrogs were croaking.
   The horses were neighing,
   The mantises praying.
   The penguins were sliding,
   The ostriches hiding.
   The rabbits were hopping.
   The pigs were slopping.
   The monkeys were swinging.
   Koalas were clinging.
   The pandas were sitting.
   The camels were spitting.
They were as bored as bored could be.
"Come home," I said. "Come home
with me."

The other day I went to the zoo.
I don't know why I went to the zoo.
It was a silly thing to do.

The wolves were howling.
The lions were growling.
The peacocks were posing,
The elephants hosing.
The tigers were crouching,
The kangaroos pouching.
The beavers were slapping.
The seals were clapping.
The hippos were soaking.
The bullfrogs were croaking.
The horses were neighing,
The mantises praying.
The penguins were sliding,
The ostriches hiding.
The rabbits were hopping.
The pigs were slopping.
The monkeys were swinging.
Koalas were clinging.
The pandas were sitting.
The camels were spitting.

They were as noisy and bored as could be.
"It's time," I said, "to come home
with me."

So two by two and three by three
I took the animals home with me.

As soon as the furniture started to break,
I knew I had made a big mistake.
They were sitting and spitting,
　　swinging and clinging,
　　hopping and slopping,
　　sliding and hiding,
　　neighing and praying,
　　soaking and croaking,
　　slapping and clapping,
　　crouching and pouching,
　　posing and hosing,
　　howling and growling.
They were as messy as messy could be.
They couldn't, they shouldn't be home
with me!

So three by three,
And two by two,

I took the animals back to the zoo.

I don't know why I went to the zoo.
It was a *wonderful* thing to do.